*To Tick, John, and Rosalie*

# EZRA JACK KEATS

# THE
# SNOWY
# DAY

PUFFIN BOOKS

Penguin Books Ltd, Harmondsworth, Middlesex, England
Penguin Books, 40 West 23rd Street, New York, New York 10010, U.S.A.
Penguin Books Australia Ltd, Ringwood, Victoria, Australia
Penguin Books Canada Limited, 2801 John Street, Markham, Ontario, Canada L3R 1B4
Penguin Books (N.Z.) Ltd, 182-190 Wairau Road, Auckland 10, New Zealand

First published by The Viking Press 1962
Viking Seafarer Edition published 1972
Reprinted 1974, 1975
Published in Puffin Books 1976
Reprinted 1977, 1978, 1980, 1981, 1982, 1983, 1984

Library of Congress Cataloging in Publication Data
Keats, Ezra Jack.     The snow day.
Summary: The adventures of a little boy in the city
on a very snowy day.
[1. Snow—Fiction]     I. Title.
[PZ7.K2253Sn8]     [E]     76-28805
ISBN 0-14-050182-7

Printed in the United States of America
Set in Bembo

One winter morning Peter woke up
and looked out the window. Snow
had fallen during the night. It cov-
ered everything as far as he could see.

After breakfast he put on his snowsuit and ran outside. The snow was piled up very high along the street to make a path for walking.

Crunch, crunch, crunch, his feet sank into the snow.
He walked with his toes pointing out, like this:

He walked with his toes
pointing in, like that:

Then he dragged his feet s-l-o-w-l-y
to make tracks.

And he found something sticking out
of the snow that made a new track.

It was a stick

— a stick that was just right for smacking a snow-covered tree.

Down fell the snow —
plop!
— on top of Peter's head.

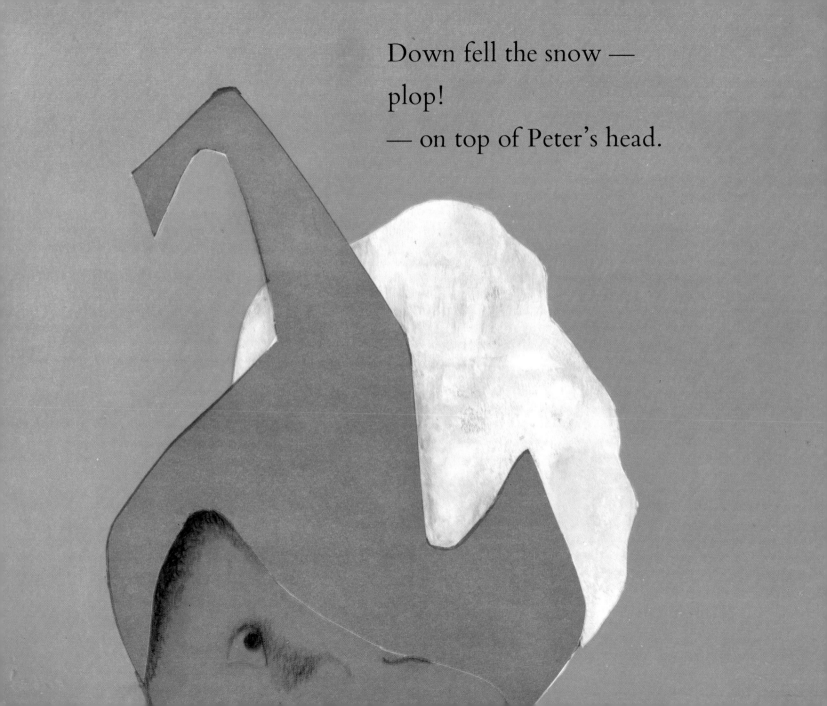

He thought it would be fun to join the big boys in their snowball fight, but he knew he wasn't old enough — not yet.

So he made a smiling snowman,

and he made angels.

He pretended
he was a mountain-climber.
He climbed up
a great big tall
heaping mountain of snow —

and slid all the way down.

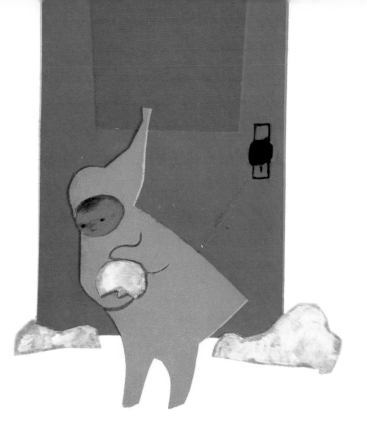

He picked up a handful of snow — and another, and still another. He packed it round and firm and put the snowball in his pocket for tomorrow. Then he went into his warm house.

He told his mother all about his adventures
while she took off his wet socks.

And he thought and thought
and thought about them.

Before he got into bed he looked in his pocket.
His pocket was empty. The snowball wasn't there.
He felt very sad.

While he slept, he dreamed that the sun
had melted all the snow away.

But when he woke up his dream was gone.

The snow was still everywhere.

New snow was falling!

After breakfast he called to his
friend from across the hall, and
they went out together into the
deep, deep snow.